# THE PAINTING GORILLA

## Michael Rex

Henry Holt and Company • New York

Henry Holt and Company, Inc., *Publishers since 1866*
115 West 18th Street, New York, New York 10011
Henry Holt is a registered trademark of Henry Holt and Company, Inc.
Copyright © 1997 by Michael Rex. All rights reserved.
Published in Canada by Fitzhenry & Whiteside Ltd.,
195 Allstate Parkway, Markham, Ontario L3R 4T8.

Library of Congress Cataloging-in-Publication Data
Rex, Michael. The painting gorilla / Michael Rex.
Summary: A gorilla who lives in a zoo and loves to paint becomes
rich and famous from her art and asks the other animals what she
should do with her money.
[ 1. Gorilla—Fiction. 2. Artists—Fiction. 3. Zoos—Fiction.
4. Zoo animals—Fiction. 5. Money—Fiction.] I. Title.
PZ7.R32875Pai 1997 [E]—dc20 96-44209

ISBN 0-8050-5020-5/ First Edition—1997
Typography by Martha Rago
The artist used acrylic on cel vinyl to create the illustrations for this book.
Printed in the United States of America on acid-free paper.∞
10 9 8 7 6 5 4 3 2 1

To my mother,
for letting me draw

—M.R.

There once was a big hairy gorilla
who made bright and beautiful paintings.

She lived in a zoo and painted
pictures of the other zoo animals.

She painted the elephant taking a bath,

the lion
taking a nap,

the hippo eating
lunch, and...

...the penguins playing tag.

She also made paintings of the people
who came to see the animals.

She painted girls holding balloons,
boys eating ice cream,

fathers taking pictures, and mothers carrying babies.

People loved the gorilla's wonderful paintings

so much that they began to buy them.

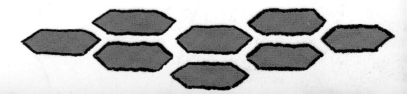

Her paintings were sent all over the world
and hung in many fascinating places.

The gorilla became very famous.

She sold so many paintings she soon had a million dollars.

But what does a gorilla need money for?

A gorilla doesn't
need expensive toys

or fancy clothes.

A gorilla doesn't need a racecar,
an airplane, or a speedboat.

And a gorilla certainly doesn't need a mini-submarine,

or an intergalactic
rocket!

So what's a gorilla
to do?

She decided to ask her friends for help.

"If you had a million dollars," she asked, "what would you buy?"

"Tall trees to swing in!" said the chimpanzee.

"Big rivers to swim in!" said the hippo.

"Miles of sand to run on!" said the ostrich.

"Fields of grass to roam in!"
said the lion.

"Water as far as the eye can see!"
said the seal.

The gorilla thought for
a moment. Then she
knew exactly what
to buy!

She bought the entire zoo and turned it into a giant playground.

Then she took all the animals back to their natural homes and...

...she set them free!